Georgia Edmonds

Copyright© 2022 by Georgia Edmonds 2022
Cover art and interior illustrations copyright© by Jake Biggin 2022
Visit Teddy at
www.teddys-tails.com

All Rights Reserved

The rights of the author and illustrator have been asserted in accordance with Sections 77 and 78 of the Copyright Designs and Patents Act, 1988.
No part of this book or its illustrations may be reproduced (including photocopying or storing in any medium by electronic means and whether or not transiently or incidentally to some other use of this publication) without the written permission of the copyright holder except in accordance with the provisions of the Copyright, Design and Patents Act 1988.

GE - For Janet, an exceptional mother, grannie and friend.

JB - For Sam and Alice and whoever has my other sock.....

Teddy Versus the Underwear!

Written by Georgia Edmonds
Illustrated by Jake Biggin

Girls, Boys and grown ups, ARE YOU READY
To hear a funny tale about a
puppy named Teddy?

Some of Teddy's escapades are really most hilarious. This PLUCKY little puppy is both loving and gregarious!

Teddy had developed a super-secret habit;
if he saw underwear,
he simply had to grab it!

So with great delight,
he gathered new possessions!

Vests, tights, (even PJ's)
were his favourite new obsessions!

His family had no idea that this was going on,
but when they couldn't find their undies,
they knew *something* must be wrong!

What was happening? What was at play?
Would yet *another* pair of socks
go missing today?

Mum had placed them all in the washing machine, to make sure their underwear was super-fresh and clean.

One minute they were folded and neatly stacked. Then suddenly they vanished! Would they ever come back?! Whatever had happened to their pants, socks and vests? What would the family wear on their bottoms, feet and chests??!

They would have to discover where
their underclothes were hiding;
so they looked around their home
to see if they could find them!

Our mischievous Teddy had used all of his skill,
to make sure the clothes
were hidden super-well!!

What would Mum, Dad and Sasha wear when they
went out? No pants on is not funny,
of that there is no doubt!

"Any luck yet?" Mum asked Sasha and Dad.
"No! Not a sign anywhere! This is looking rather bad!"

A clever idea sprang into Sasha's mind,
as he remembered what Teddy always liked to find..

"Teddy come here!" And his puppy trotted up,
"I think that you have been a very a cheeky pup!
Could it be you who is our clothing Thief?
Are you hiding our vests, socks and briefs?!"
Teddy barked,"Woof!" and ran to his bed.
"What will I find in there, little Ted?"

Teddy woofed again and jumped on his bedcover...Underneath the blanket, what would they discover?!
Teddy pushed the blanket back with his nose....
What was hiding beneath, do you suppose?

YES! In Teddy's bed they found their missing underwear ...
pants, vests and socks; were all lying there!

"We have to put these items back;
when we get dressed,
this is clothing we can't lack!

Here is a favourite toy I haven't cuddled in a while..

It's a blue bear called Fred
and he always made me smile!

So this is a toy for you to keep.
To snuggle in your bed when you go to sleep!"

Teddy rolled on his back with his paws in the air!
Fred was far more snuggly
than the missing underwear!

With their lost clothes recovered,
the mystery was solved!

With help from Sasha,
all had been resolved!

The family, of their puppy
had a whole new perception...
They had been part of Teddy's
GREAT UNDERWEAR DECEPTION..

TWO little "TEDDYS" WERE now TOGETHER -
SO THEY CAN BE
BEST-BEAR FRIENDS FUR-EVER!

THE EN

This first book in the Teddy's Tails series is also available on Amazon
(direct link via www.teddy's-tails.com)

In this delightful story he meets some new friends... THE TYGERS! This encounter has both entertaining and amusing consequences! Children will enjoy the verse and rhythm of the story following the hilarious, antics of Teddy, as he navigates new friendships.

Printed in Great Britain
by Amazon